A Note from the Author

So, it is ten years since the Gruffalo's Child first set foot in the snowy wood in search of the Big Bad Mouse, while her father snored in the Gruffalo cave. (I often get asked about the whereabouts of her mother. The answer is: I just don't know; not everything is revealed to authors.)

The Gruffalo had already been in print for five years when the sequel came out. I had never really intended to write one, that is until I started to wonder what the Gruffalo would think of the mouse five years on. Would he have cottoned on to the fact that he'd been duped? Surely not, being a beast of brawn rather than brain. I decided that it was far more likely that the mouse would have grown to epic proportions in his mind; and then I began to wonder what would happen if another gruffalo sought out the mythical "Big Bad Mouse". Initially I had envisaged a whole caveful of little gruffalos (or should it be gruffali?) of whom only one was brave enough to undertake the quest, but the publisher talked me out of this idea, and now it feels inconceivable that the Gruffalo should have more than one child.

Axel Scheffler's illustrations to this story are among my favourites of all his work, which is saying a lot. I love all the playful details he has added, like the idea of giving the Gruffalo's Child some stick toys, and the snow gruffalo that the mouse has built.

So, now that the Gruffalo's Child has reached double figures, I would like to thank Axel for giving her shape and form, and to wish *her* Many Happy Returns.

Julia Donaldson

THE GRUFFALO'S CHILD

Julia Donaldson

Illustrated by Axel Scheffler

Macmillan Children's Books

The Gruffalo said that no gruffalo should
Ever set foot in the deep dark wood.
"Why not? Why not?" *"Because if you do*
The Big Bad Mouse will be after you.
I met him once," said the Gruffalo.
"I met him a long long time ago."

"What does he look like? Tell us, Dad.
Is he terribly big and terribly bad?"

"I can't quite remember," the Gruffalo said.
Then he thought for a minute and scratched his head.

"The Big Bad Mouse is terribly strong
And his scaly tail is terribly long.

His eyes are like pools of terrible fire
And his terrible whiskers are tougher than wire."

One snowy night when the Gruffalo snored
The Gruffalo's Child was feeling bored.

The Gruffalo's Child was feeling brave
So she tiptoed out of the gruffalo cave.
The snow fell fast and the wind blew wild.
Into the wood went the Gruffalo's Child.

Aha! Oho! A trail in the snow!
Whose is this trail and where does it go?
A tail poked out of a logpile house.
Could this be the tail of the Big Bad Mouse?

Out slid the creature. His eyes were small
And he didn't have whiskers – no, none at all.

"You're not the Mouse." *"Not I,"* said the snake.
"He's down by the lake – eating gruffalo cake."

The snow fell fast and the wind blew wild.
"I'm not scared," said the Gruffalo's Child.

Aha! Oho! Marks in the snow!
Whose are these claw marks? Where do they go?
Two eyes gleamed out of a treetop house.
Could these be the eyes of the Big Bad Mouse?

Down flew the creature. His tail was short
And he didn't have whiskers of any sort.

"You're not the Mouse." *"Toowhoo, not I,*
But he's somewhere nearby, eating gruffalo pie."

The snow fell fast and the wind blew wild.
"I'm not scared," said the Gruffalo's Child.

Aha! Oho! A track in the snow!
Whose is this track and where does it go?
Whiskers at last! And an underground house!
Could this be the home of the Big Bad Mouse?

Out slunk the creature. His eyes weren't fiery.
His tail wasn't scaly. His whiskers weren't wiry.

"You're not the Mouse." *"Oh no, not me.*
He's under a tree – drinking gruffalo tea."

"It's all a trick!" said the Gruffalo's Child
As she sat on a stump where the snow lay piled.
"I don't *believe* in the Big Bad Mouse . . .

"But here comes a little one, out of his house!
Not big, not bad, but a mouse at least –
You'll taste good as a midnight feast."

"*Wait!*" said the mouse. "*Before you eat,*
There's a friend of mine that you ought to meet.
If you'll let me hop onto a hazel twig
I'll beckon my friend so bad and big."

The Gruffalo's Child unclenched her fist.
"The Big Bad Mouse – so he *does* exist!"
The mouse hopped into the hazel tree.
He beckoned, then said, *"Just wait and see."*

Out came the moon. It was bright and round.
A terrible shadow fell onto the ground.

Who is this creature so big, bad and strong?
His tail and his whiskers are terribly long.
His ears are enormous, and over his shoulder
He carries a nut as big as a boulder!

"The Big Bad Mouse!" yelled the Gruffalo's Child.
The mouse jumped down from the twig and smiled.

Aha! Oho! Prints in the snow.

Whose are these footprints? Where do they go?

The footprints led to the gruffalo cave

Where the Gruffalo's Child was a bit less brave.

The Gruffalo's Child was a bit less bored . . .

And the Gruffalo snored and snored and snored.

For Franzeska – J.D.
For Freya and Cora – A.S.

First published 2004 by Macmillan Children's Books
This edition published 2014 by Macmillan Children's Books
a division of Macmillan Publishers Limited
20 New Wharf Road, London N1 9RR
Basingstoke and Oxford
Associated companies throughout the world
www.panmacmillan.com

ISBN: 978-1-4472-7363-9

Text copyright © Julia Donaldson 2004, 2014
Illustrations copyright © Axel Scheffler 2004, 2014
Moral rights asserted.

3 5 7 9 8 6 4 2

A CIP catalogue record for this book is available from the British Library.

Printed in China

A Note from the Illustrator

A few years after *The Gruffalo* was published, I found out that he was going to have a child – or as I first thought, children. When I read the story of *The Gruffalo's Child* I imagined more than one child, and so on my very first sketches there are three little gruffalos. But in the end, his daughter turned out to be an only child, so I drew her a stick doll to keep her company. (In case you're wondering, it isn't *the* Stick Man, just a distant relative, but it did inspire Julia to write *Stick Man* a few years later.)

I was very worried when I realised the story was set at night, in a very dark, very cold winter wood. Would I be able to draw and paint that? Luckily it turned out to be easier than I thought. The greatest challenge actually turned out to be the shadow of the Big Bad Mouse in the snow. Somehow it looks real in the book – even though it defies all the laws of physics! But then maybe picture books have their own logic: there would never be a snake in the snow because they hibernate in the winter, yet there he is! That's why I gave him sleepy eyes, so it looks as though the Gruffalo's Child has just wakened him in the middle of his hibernation.

But the first thing I had to think about was what a gruffalo would look like as a child. Would she already have horns? Yes, I decided – small and round. The eyes I made yellow instead of orange, and the purple prickles became small and pink. No poisonous wart or knobbly knees – they come later, maybe when the little gruffalo becomes a teenager. In the meantime, she remains ever-young within the pages of her book, and will still look exactly the same in another ten years!

Axel Scheffler